THIS WALKER BOOK BELONGS TO:

LITTLE
SO-AND-SO
and the
DINOSAURS

Written by
DAVID LLOYD

Illustrated by
PETER CROSS

WALKER BOOKS
LONDON

To Timothy and Emily-Mei
P.C.

First published individually as
Early Morning, Breakfast,
The Terrible Thing and *Silly Games*
in 1985 by Walker Books Ltd
87 Vauxhall Walk, London SE11 5HJ

This edition published 1993

Reprinted 1993

Printed and bound in Great Britain by
Ebenezer Baylis Ltd, Worcester

British Library Cataloguing in Publication Data
A catalogue record for this book is available from the British Library.
ISBN 0-7445-2029-0

⋀⋀ CONTENTS ⋀⋀

CHAPTER ONE
EARLY MORNING

The dinosaurs
were sleeping.
The only sound was
their gentle breathing.

hoooOOSh
wOOOSh

The sun rose.
The dinosaurs
woke up.

Ummmhummmm

They hummed softly.

oooooooo oo aaaaaaaa

There was an egg.
It was under So-So-Slowly.

criCK
craCK

The egg hatched.

Out jumped
Little So-and-So.

Little So-and-So spotted the sun.

It was over the mountains.

He wanted to eat it.

He found the sun.
It was in the water.
He jumped on it.

splash

OOOOOOOooooooo

The mountains stood up.
They turned into
Rock-a-bye.

Under
Rock-a-bye
there were
babies everywhere.

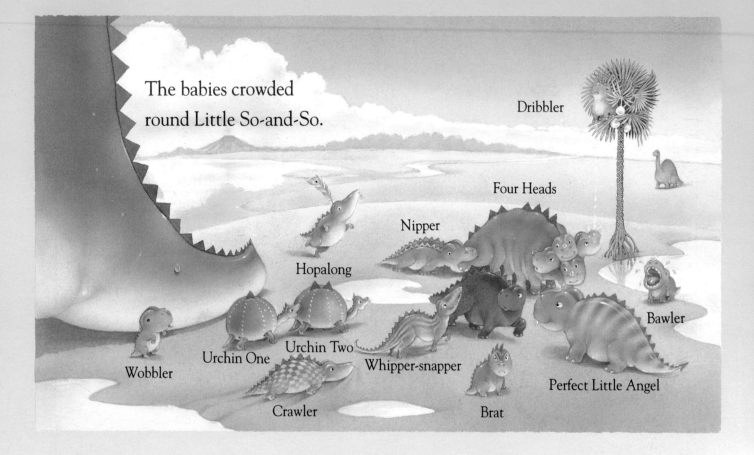

The babies crowded round Little So-and-So.

Dribbler

Four Heads

Nipper

Hopalong

Wobbler

Urchin One

Urchin Two

Whipper-snapper

Crawler

Brat

Bawler

Perfect Little Angel

smaCK

Perfect Little Angel kissed Little So-and-So.

Suddenly the earth
began to shake.

Water flew everywhere.
Rock-a-bye was shaking
the water off his back.

Little So-and-So
looked up.
He saw rainbows.
So-So-Slowly was there.
Goodbye, Rock-a-bye.
It's time to go.

So-So-Slowly set out for breakfast.

trump trump trump

Little So-and-So rode on her back.

bump bump bump

Little So-and-So fell off.

He ran about.

He fell into a footprint.

booph

12

They came to the forest.

crunch munch crunch

The leaves were too high up for Little So-and-So.

A leaf floated down, and another, then more and more.

Snip snap

One leaf flew away.

It was a butterfly.
Little So-and-So
chased it.
He never saw
all the creatures
in the forest.

But they saw him.
They followed him.

Rotter

Softy

Dotty

Lazybones

Jelly Bug

Sneak

Busybody

Pipsqueak

Slowcoach

Show-off

Creep

Fuzz-buzz

wheeeeeeeeeeeeeeee....

Little So-and-So slid
and rolled down
and down
and
down.

**wham
bam**

He bumped
into the
boomer.

The boomer rolled him over.
They all rolled him over.

They rolled
him over

and over

and over

back to So-So-Slowly.

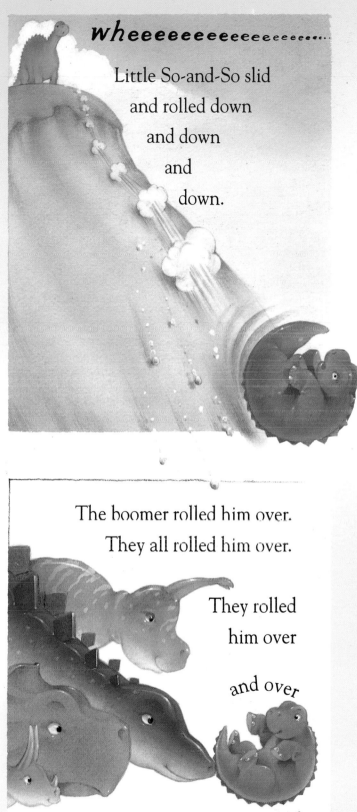

19

Everyone licked the stones.
The taste was salty.
Little So-and-So
licked a stone.

hoo ha

The taste made
him happy.

*hoo ha
hoo hic hoc*

Little So-and-So
was the noisiest
of all the noisy
dinosaurs.

rrrrrrrrrrr r r r r

Shhhhhhhhhhhhhhhhhhh

Look out for the
terrible thing!

The dinosaurs
were frightened.
They tried to look

big

small

hurt

hidden

horrible to eat

very, very frightening.

ha
hoO hic hoC

Only Little So-and-So
carried on being noisy.

ROARrrrrrrrr
rrrrrrR
R
R
R
R
R
R

The terrible thing
made a terrible noise when
it saw Little So-and-So.

Little So-and-So
closed his eyes.

Urrrrrrrrgh

The terrible thing
went away.

Everyone was happy again.
Everyone was safe.

hoot
hiss
hiccup
honk
boom
hooha
hichoc
umhummmmmm~

Goodbye, noisy dinosaurs.
It's time to go.

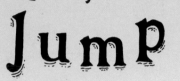
Little So-and-So
was being silly.

Jumpetty

Jumpetty

Jump

He bounced on
So-So-Slowly's tummy.

So-So-Slowly
rolled over.
Little So-and-So danced
onto her nose.

hoppity
hoppity
hop

So-So-Slowly stood up.
ₒₒₒₒₒₒₒₒₒₒₒₒₒₒₒₒₒₒₒₒₒₒₒₒₒₒₒₒₒₒₒₒₒₒ O O O O O O O
It was a long, long way
to the ground.

So-So-Slowly strode
across the world.

Little So-and-So
raced and chased
around her feet.

ohhhhhhhhhhhh

They saw Atlas,
the giant mountain turtle.

ahhhhhhhhhhhh

They saw little
Eohippus.

They came to
the water-hole.

gurgle slurp

The dinosaurs
were drinking.

So-So-Slowly sucked in
gallons of water.
Her cheeks were
green balloons.

shooowhh

So-So-Slowly blew
out the water,
just for fun.

Little So-and-So
blew water at
High-and-Mighty.

phht phtt

hmph

High-and-Mighty
was not
amused.

So-So-Slowly took
Little So-and-So away.

The last rays of the sun
shone softly on the dinosaurs.

Good night, So-So-Slowly.
Good night, Little So-and-So.
It's time to sleep.

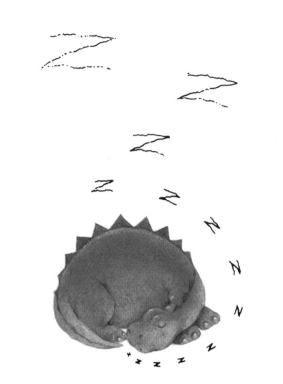

THE END

MORE WALKER PAPERBACKS
For You to Enjoy

Also by David Lloyd

THE BALL
illustrated by Mary Rees

Follow the bouncing progress of a ball and the children who pursue it.

"A book to look out for... Excellent." *Parents*

0-7445-2017-7   £3.99

THE SNEEZE
illustrated by Fritz Wegner

Take a girl, a dog and a man. Add a suitcase, a hat, a ball,
a newspaper and a seat in the park. Mix them all up and make a story!

"A real treat ... elegant, pretty, wildly funny and rousing...
not to be missed." *Naomi Lewis, The Observer*

0-7445-1784-2   £2.99

HELLO, GOODBYE
illustrated by Louise Voce

First there is just a tree. Then a bear comes along, then a bee, then
all sorts of other animals appear – and disappear!

"Wonderful story... Bright, simple illustrations... A good book
to use as a reading aid and great for the young child, too."
Nursery World

0-7445-1348-0   £3.99

CAT AND DOG
illustrated by Clive Scruton

A bold and breathless chase. Perfect for young readers.

0-7445-1317-0   £3.99

**Walker Paperbacks are available from most booksellers, or by post from
Walker Books Ltd, PO Box 11, Falmouth, Cornwall TR10 9EN.**

To order, send: Title, author, ISBN number and price for each book ordered, your full name and address, cheque or postal order
for the total amount, plus postage and packing: UK and BFPO Customers – £1.00 for first book, plus 50p for the second book
and plus 30p for each additional book to a maximum charge of £3.00. Overseas and Eire Customers – £2.00 for first book,
plus £1.00 for the second book and plus 50p per copy for each additional book.
Prices are correct at time of going to press, but are subject to change without notice.